Bartholomew's Gift

Written by
Diane Dignan

FERNE PRESS

Illustrated by
Wendy Edelson

Bartholomew's Gift
Copyright © 2010 by Diane Dignan
Illustrations by Wendy Edelson
Layout and cover design by Kimberly Franzen
Printed in the United States of America

Summary: Bartholomew receives a unique gift at birth, but loses it as he grows older, only to find that perhaps it wasn't lost after all.

Illustrations created using watercolors.

Library of Congress Cataloging-in-Publication Data
  Dignan, Diane
  Bartholomew's Gift /Diane Dignan – First Edition
  ISBN-13: 978-1-933916-56-9
  1. Gift book. 2. Fiction. 3. Angels. 4. Faith.
  I. Dignan, Diane II. Bartholomew's Gift
  Library of Congress Control Number: 2010926937

FERNE PRESS

Ferne Press is an imprint of Nelson Publishing & Marketing
366 Welch Road, Northville, MI 48167
www.nelsonpublishingandmarketing.com
(248) 735-0418

The following individuals contributed their unique and wonderful creative talents to the publication of this story. Thank you for bringing Bartholomew's Gift to life:

Recording engineered by Randy Leipnik of Semper Media Group
www.sempermediagroup.com

Narration performed by Lecia Macryn

"Cherished in His Eyes" harp and arrangement by Charles Walker

"Cherished in His Eyes" sung by Nancy Oz

The following music written and performed by Kevin MacLeod:
"Eternal Hope"
"Frozen Star"
"Sovereign"
"Two Together"
"Feelin' Good"
"Continue Life"

This book is dedicated to Jim. You are my angel on earth.

Cherish:
To care for, watch over, treasure, and dearly love.

When Bartholomew was born, he received a special gift. It was gentler than the warm, comfy blanket his mother cuddled around him. It was more lasting than the shining silver cup he would learn to drink from. The gift was there, secret, unknown to everyone but him.

Bartholomew grew and began to toddle about the house. As he sat on his bedroom floor playing with colored blocks, his mother saw him stretch his arms upward, asking to be lifted, though no one was there. During naptime, she heard him talking baby prattle while alone in his crib.

"Bartholomew has an imaginary playmate," his mother said to his father that evening over dinner.

"That's nice," his father said. "He'll outgrow it eventually."

When Bartholomew grew big enough to ride his bicycle all by himself, his gift remained. At times, he would see a pretty lady in a long white gown glowing like the full moon on a dark night. He would see the golden wings folded behind her.

"Why couldn't Mommy and Daddy see her standing right beside them?" he wondered. The beautiful lady would wink at him as she put her finger to her lips and said, "Shh."

Leaning close to Mommy or Daddy, she would sing a sweet song to them before disappearing from sight. Her song went like this:

"This song is placed
inside your heart
so you may realize
God's forever love for you.
You're cherished
in His eyes."

Sometimes, as he fell asleep, Bartholomew heard the song, soft and delicate, in his ear. His special friend would brush her fingertips across his cheek. He would draw the covers closer, smile, and fall asleep—glad that she was near.

The beautiful lady with glistening wings came to Bartholomew's house many times. When going places with his parents or visiting friends, he noticed other people dressed in glowing white with beautiful wings. No one else was aware of them. Bartholomew decided that people must be too busy to notice.

On a snowy winter night, Bartholomew's family went into town
shopping. Crisp snow crunched under foot as they hurried past the park.
A nativity scene was placed there with soft light shining down upon it. He saw Mary,
Joseph, and the baby Jesus. Over the manger was a lady with a white dress and golden wings!

"Look!" Bartholomew said and pointed excitedly at the lady.

"Yes, dear, that's an angel," his mother replied. "Angels are God's messengers and are all around us, though no one can see them."

All at once Bartholomew understood who these sparkling people were and that they are invisible. It was as if he had finally opened the gift given to him at birth and peered inside. He could see and hear angels!

When Bartholomew was eight years old, his mother and father gave him a sister. He loved to watch his mother rock little Sarah to sleep while singing softly to her. The pretty lady would stand close to Mommy and Sarah, wrapping her wings around them. That made Bartholomew very happy. One evening, as Mommy rocked and sang to Sarah, the angel's song came from Mommy's lips.

*"This song is placed
inside your heart
so you may realize
God's forever love for you.
You're cherished
in His eyes."*

Bartholomew could hardly believe his ears! Mommy must have seen his special friend and heard her lovely song.

In his excitement, he asked his mother, "Did the shining lady teach you that song, Mommy?"

His mother looked at him strangely and said, "I don't know what you are talking about, Bartholomew. I have never seen a shining lady and haven't heard any music."

"Oh," was all Bartholomew said.

But his question seemed to have made his mother sad.

Later that night, when his parents thought he was asleep, Bartholomew hid in the hallway and listened as they talked.

His father said, "Do you think he needs to see a specialist? He's getting much too old for this invisible playmate nonsense."

"Let's give it a while," said his mother. "Perhaps it will go away."

Bartholomew decided then and there, he would not mention seeing angels ever again. Still, on days when his mother was too tired to smile at him or his father would quietly sit alone at the end of the day, the angel would appear. Bartholomew felt warm and peaceful as the angel rested her hand on his parents' shoulders or sang her beautiful song. She smiled or spoke to Bartholomew at every visit. He knew she was his very own angel, and that she loved him and his family very much.

Bartholomew's days became full of learning and homework, baseball and music, friends and television. He slowly forgot about the beautiful lady and her song. Like a vapor that vanishes when the sunlight shines upon it, Bartholomew's angel slowly faded away amid the activity of his life.

Sometimes when the days slowed down to night and he was just dozing off to sleep, he thought he heard her voice calling his name.

"Bartholomew. Bartholomew, dear, don't forget...

This song is placed
inside your heart
so you may realize
God's forever love for you.
You're cherished
in His eyes."

The years went by, and Bartholomew became a teenager. His mind was full of studies and sports, cars and friends. He never told his friends about his unique gift. They would think he was weird or, worse yet, stop being his friends altogether. Besides, all that angel stuff was for kids. Now that he was growing up, he no longer saw the shining lady or heard her song. He began to believe that perhaps his little-kid mind had made the whole thing up.

Eventually, Bartholomew grew up to be a fine man with a wife named Annie. He worked long hours to earn enough money so they could start a family. Many evenings he came home very tired and sat by himself like his father had done when Bartholomew was a little boy. Yet even during those quiet times, he no longer heard a soft voice whispering in his ear. He had misplaced his gift somewhere among the clutter and activity of his adult life.

Then one day, Annie gave birth to a baby boy. She and Bartholomew named him Nathaniel. Bartholomew loved to watch Annie rock Nathaniel to sleep and sing tender lullabies to him. At those moments, he felt very happy.

One cozy winter evening as he watched Annie rock Nathaniel, a beautiful thing happened. Bartholomew found his lost gift! Suddenly he saw his angel, glowing like the petals of a white rose in sunshine, approach the rocking chair. She smiled at him, lifted her finger to her lips, and said, "Shh."

Then she wrapped her golden wings around Annie and the baby, and she began to sing:

"This song is placed
inside your heart
so you may realize
God's forever love for you.
You're cherished in His eyes.
Cherished in His eyes are you,
cherished in His eyes.
God will never leave your side.
You're cherished in His eyes."

Nathaniel wriggled and cooed in his blanket. Then he reached up and touched the angel's face with his tiny hand.

"Annie," Bartholomew whispered. "There's an angel hugging you and the baby."

Annie looked around the chair, glancing this way and that.

"I don't see her," she said, "but I believe you."

Bartholomew sat back in his chair and gave a wink to his angel friend. She winked back at him and smiled, and he knew—she had been with him all along.

Cherished in His Eyes

Diane Dignan

This song is placed in-side your heart so you may re - a - lize God's for-e - ver

love for you. You're cher - ished in His eyes. Cher - ished in His eyes are you,

cher - ished in His eyes. God will nev - er leave your side. You're cher - ished in His eyes.